PUFFIN BOOKS

SOMETHING I REMEMBER

I'll tell you, shall I, something I remember? Something that still means a great deal to me. It was long ago . . .

Eleanor Farjeon's poetry captures the whole of the child's world with both perception and charm. Her sharpness of sense, her emotional insight, her warmth and her lively humour give her rich and varied poetry a unique appeal for both children and adults. This is the first major collection of Eleanor Farjeon's poetry for years and contains not only some of her most popular poems but also some of her lesser known works that have been long out of print.

Eleanor Farjeon was born in 1882 and wrote her first poem at the age of six. She wrote both stories and poetry prolifically, and some of her best known works include *The Little Bookroom*, *The Old Nurse's Stocking-Basket* and *Kings and Queens* (written with her brother, Herbert).

Anne Harvey's interest in poetry also began at an early age and she has enjoyed Eleanor Farjeon's poetry since childhood. She originally trained at the Guildhall School of Music and Drama and now combines her work as a director and performer with freelance writing, lecturing, broadcasting and adjudicating at poetry and drama festivals. Her other books in Puffin include *Of Caterpillars, Cats and Cattle*, *Poets in Hand – A Puffin Quintet* and *Six of the Best – A Puffin Sextet*.

Another book by Eleanor Farjeon

The Little Bookroom

Eleanor and Herbert Farjeon

Kings and Queens

Something I Remember

Selected poems for children by
Eleanor Farjeon

Edited by Anne Harvey

Illustrated by Alan Marks

Puffin Books

To Primrose Lockwood and the children of Marlcliffe School because they
like Eleanor Farjeon so much

PUFFIN BOOKS

Published by the Penguin Group
27 Wrights Lane, London W8 5TZ, England
Viking Penguin Inc., 40 West 23rd Street, New York, New York 10010, USA
Penguin Books Australia Ltd, Ringwood, Victoria, Australia
Penguin Books Canada Ltd, 2801 John Street, Markham, Ontario, Canada L3R 1B4
Penguin Books (NZ) Ltd, 182–190 Wairau Road, Auckland 10, New Zealand

Penguin Books Ltd, Registered Offices: Harmondsworth, Middlesex, England

First published by Blackie and Son Ltd 1987
Published in Puffin Books 1989
10 9 8 7 6 5 4 3 2 1

Copyright © Gervase Farjeon
This collection copyright © Anne Harvey, 1987
Illustrations copyright © Alan Marks, 1987
All rights reserved

Printed and bound in Great Britain by
Cox & Wyman Ltd, Reading

INTRODUCTION

Eleanor Farjeon once said that she was singing songs before she could write, and even before she could speak, and as soon as she could guide a pencil she began to write them down. Words were always a delight to her, and when other children were playing outside she would be hunched over a book reading or scribbling stories and poems.

She never went to school. Her father told her governess: 'Don't teach my children anything they don't wish to learn.' Of course Eleanor and her three brothers did have lessons, but they were given plenty of freedom in their London nursery, and much of it was spent in imaginative play. They were taken to pantomimes, plays and concerts. They met the actors, writers and musicians who were their parents' friends.

B. L. Farjeon (Ben) was a writer himself, and gave Eleanor a good deal of encouragement. When she had written something she would quickly slide it under his study door, then run to her room to await his comments. Uneven lines, carelessness, poor use of words would not escape his sharp eyes.

An important day was when Papa came to her room, having just read her latest story. He stood by her bed a moment, then told her: 'I have hopes of you, Nell. I think you're going to be a writer one day.'

More than anything else, Eleanor wanted to please her father.

Eleanor was a very romantic child. She was born on 13 February 1881, when Queen Victoria was on the throne, and she wished it had been just one day later, St Valentine's Day. She wished, too, that she was as pretty as her dainty American mother, and not short-sighted, straight-haired and clumsy.

At parties she used to meet a golden-haired, blue-eyed, light-footed girl called Olive, and envied her. Eleanor was always painfully shy at parties. She couldn't relax and enjoy the games and chatter. One dreadful party memory remained with her all her life. After tea the children were asked to sing, dance or recite to entertain each other, and she was so nervous that all the words of her poem went clean out of her head. After the third attempt, she ran along the polished floor to her mother, tears streaming behind her glasses, while little Olive got up and pirouetted like a fairy.

At home she wasn't shy at all, and was always ready to dress up, dance and sing, and act out whatever stories her elder brother, Harry, chose. Harry was very much the leader of the nursery. Their mother once said to the children: 'I never had any trouble bringing you up. I left all that to Harry.' He made decisions, and rules for sharing, fair-play, cleanliness, manners and bed-time. No argument was allowed.

'Bed-time, Joe and Bertie,' he would announce, glancing at his watch at 8.30 pm. His young brothers might be playing Ludo.

'Can't we just have—'

'Bed-time! Good-night!'

Eleanor was sixteen years old before she dared to disobey Harry over her 9.30 pm bedtime, and nervous about his reaction. But she adored him and always looked up to him.

Ben Farjeon died when Eleanor was twenty, and she began writing seriously for her living. As she started to publish successfully she grew less shy, and soon made friends outside her family. She found that more and more people turned to her for advice when they had problems and the writers amongst them valued her judgement over their work.

Joe and Bertie became writers, too, and Harry a very clever music teacher. Eleanor used to help him give parties for his younger pupils, and she was the life and soul of them, arranging food and joining in games with enthusiasm.

'Nellie, why don't you stop playing with the children, and sit down a moment?' her mother called out once. Eleanor came to with a surprise—she'd forgotten she wasn't one of the children. Later, the party games gave her ideas for poems, as you'll see in *The Mulberry Bush* section of this book.

In 1981, the year of Eleanor Farjeon's centenary, I made a radio programme about her life, and interviewed some of her friends.

'She was the best friend of every friend she ever had,' said one.

'She always found time to listen, and talk, and she was such fun,' said another.

'Eleanor was a mixture of jolly aunt and magic fairy godmother,' said a man, who, when a small boy, had spent happy hours in her Hampstead cottage, listening to stories and admiring her collection of beautiful fans and other treasures.

And everyone said, 'Of course, there were the cats!' It seemed that all the local strays knew where to come for warmth and a full saucer. Her own cats were special. 'Marmalade' she firmly informed people. 'Golden. Not ginger.'

Although Eleanor had no children of her own she loved being with them and some appear in her poems. The child in *Myfanwy Among the Leaves* is the youngest daughter of the poet, Edward Thomas. Carol, in *Girls' Names and Boys' Names* is the son of the American poet, Robert Frost. Joan, in the same poem is her niece.

The artist, James Guthrie, had three sons who thought of Eleanor as a second mother. One of them, Robin, drew pictures of her walking the countryside to go with her poem *All the Way to Alfriston*, and he is the boy of *In Goes Robin*.

The country gave her great joy, and so did Christmas; the giving and receiving of presents, the sense of occasion never lost their thrill. And the religious side was important to her, as you'll see in the Christmas section.

When Eleanor Farjeon died, aged 84, in 1965, she had published over eighty books, and won many prizes. But she never liked being interviewed or photographed.

'What do you look like?' asked a newspaper reporter over the telephone.

'Like a cheerful suet pudding!' came her reply. Giving advice once about writing for children she said: 'Make sure that what you write will have in it some first hand spark of fun, or fancy, or observation, or knowledge . . . and write what YOU will enjoy writing.'

When you read her poems, I think you will know just what she meant.

Anne Harvey

IT WAS LONG AGO

I'll tell you, shall I, something I remember?
Something that still means a great deal to me.
It was long ago.

A dusty road in summer I remember,
A mountain, and an old house, and a tree
That stood, you know,

Behind the house. An old woman I remember
In a red shawl with a grey cat on her knee
Humming under a tree.

She seemed the oldest thing I can remember,
But then perhaps I was not more than three.
It was long ago.

I dragged on the dusty road, and I remember
How the old woman looked over the fence at me
And seemed to know

How it felt to be three, and called out, I remember
'Do you like bilberries and cream for tea?'
I went under the tree

And while she hummed, and the cat purred, I remember
How she filled a saucer with berries and cream for me
So long ago,

Such berries and such cream as I remember
I never had seen before, and never see
To-day, you know.

And that is almost all I can remember,
The house, the mountain, the grey cat on her knee,
Her red shawl, and the tree,

And the taste of the berries, the feel of the sun I remember,
And the smell of everything that used to be
So long ago,

Till the heat on the road outside again I remember,
And how the long dusty road seemed to have for me
No end, you know.

That is the farthest thing I can remember.
It won't mean much to you. It does to me.
Then I grew up, you see.

DAY AND NIGHT

GOOD MORNING

Good-morning now.
Wake, body,
Wake, mind!
Work, play,
Seek, find,
Eat breakfast,
Dinner too,
Wash, brush,
Sing, dance, and do!
Good-morning now.

Oh! I have just had such a lovely dream!
And then I woke,
And all the dream went out like kettle-steam,
Or chimney-smoke.

My dream was all about—how funny, though!
I've only just
Dreamed it, and now it has begun to blow
Away like dust.

In it I went—no! in my dream I had—
No, that's not it!
I can't remember, oh, it is *too* bad,
My dream a bit.

But I saw something beautiful, I'm sure—
Then someone spoke,
And then I didn't see it any more,
Because I woke.

BREAKFAST

Is it coffee for breakfast?
I wish it was tea!
Is it jam? Oh, why can't there
Be honey for me?

Is it brown bread-and-butter?
I wish it was toast!
Is it just bread-and-milk?
I like porridge the most.

Is it soft-boiled eggs? Bother!
I'd rather have fried.
You *know* I don't like soft-boiled eggs,
Though I've tried.

Of all horrid breakfasts
This breakfast's the worst!—
Who tumbled out of his bed
Wrong leg first?

CHILD AND DOG

Hello, Towzer! what's he after?
  Cocking head all on one side,
Grinning mouth that pleads with laughter—
  Master!—not to be denied.

Lolling tongue and tail a-wagging,
  So persuasive—*master, please!*—
One ear cocked and the other flagging,
  There is no resisting these!

Quick small feet on legs a-straddle,
  Eyes with loving hopes abrim—
Master! do you *think* some lad'll
  Throw his ball and play with him?

HEEL

The sun inside me lights a flame,
The wind says everything I feel.
Life is my tremendous game!
Race? Hunt? Fight? Bark? Gobble? Steal?—
Quietly, he says my name
In *that* voice. And I come to heel.

BLISS

Let me fetch sticks,
Let me fetch stones,
Throw me your bones,
Teach me your tricks.

When you go ride,
Let me go run
You in the sun,
Me at your side;

When you go swim,
Let me go too
Both lost in blue
Up to the brim;

Let me do this,
Let me do that—
What you are at,
That is my bliss.

BRAVERY

The cow in the meadow
    Looks sideways at me—
    But what do I care?
    With my chin in the air,
I stare at the stile,
    Or a cloud, or a tree,
When the cow in the meadow
    Looks sideways at me.

The cow in the meadow
    Is not more than three,
    And you're not very bold
    When you aren't very old,
So I mustn't alarm her—
    She's *timid*, you see,
And that's why she always
    Looks sideways at me.

She gives me my milk
    And my butter for tea.
    '*Git* on!' says John,
    And at once she gits on—
And I stick to the footpath
    As brave as can be,
When the cow in the meadow
    Looks sideways at me.

THE SMOKE

Over there
Is a little house,
Quiet as a mouse,
Or an empty hive,
Or as death.
But up in the air
From the chimney-poke
Goes the gentle smoke,
And I know that the house is alive,
I can see its breath.

17

BLIND ALLEY

There's a turning I must pass
Often four times in a day,
Narrow, rather dark, with grass
Growing, a neglected way;

Two long walls, a tumbled shed,
Bushes shadowing each wall—
When I've wondered where it led
People say, Nowhere at all.

But if that is true, oh why
Should this turning be at all?
Some time, in the daylight, I
Will creep up along the wall;

For it somehow makes you think,
It has such a secret air,
It might lead you to the brink
Of—oh well, of anywhere!

Some time I will go. And see,
Here's the turning just in sight,
Full of shadows beckoning me!
Some time, yes. But not tonight.

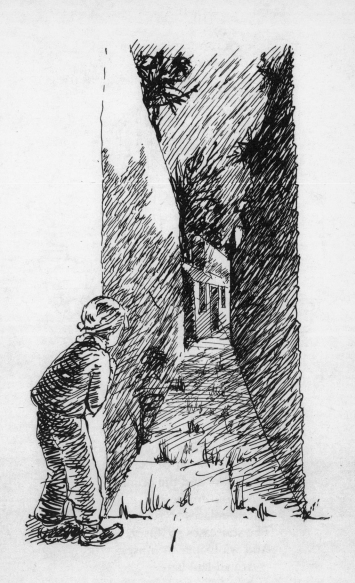

HOUSE COMING DOWN

They're pulling down the house
   At the corner of the Square,
The floors and the ceilings
   Are out in the air,
The fireplaces so rusty,
The staircases so dusty,
And wallpaper so musty,
   Are all laid bare.

It looks like a dolls' house
    With the dolls put away,
And the furniture laid by
    Against another day;
No bed to lie in,
No pan to fry in,
Or dish to make a pie in,
    And nobody to play.

That was the parlour
    With the cream-and-yellow scrawls,
That was the bedroom
    With the roses on the walls,
There's a dark red lining
In the room they had for dining,
And a brown one, rather shining,
    Goes all up the halls.

But where is the lady
    In a pretty gown?
Where is the baby
    That used to crow and frown?
Oh, the rooms look so little,
The house looks so brittle,
And no one cares a tittle
    If it all tumbles down.

BOREDOM

Oh dear! What shall I do?
Nothing lasts more than a minute or two,
Everything's silly, and nothing is fun,
And there doesn't seem anything left to be done.

Oh dear! what shall I do?
I've read all my fairy-tales seven times through,
I'm tired of my bricks and I'm sick of my train,
And my paint-box was left out all night in the rain.

Oh dear! what shall I do?
I don't *want* to go in the garden with you,
I don't *want* to sit down and play a nice game,
I want to do something that isn't the same.

Everything, everything *is* such a bore!
I don't enjoy being alive any more.
Why can't there sometimes be something that's new?
Oh dear! *what shall I* DO?

THERE ISN'T TIME!

There isn't time, there isn't time
To do the things I want to do,
With all the mountain-tops to climb,
And all the woods to wander through,
And all the seas to sail upon,
And everywhere there is to go,
And all the people, every one
Who lives upon the earth, to know.
There's only time, there's only time
To know a few, and do a few,
And then sit down and make a rhyme
About the rest I want to do.

23

EVENING HUSHES

Evening hushes
The thoughts of the Poplars, the dreams of the
Rushes.

BEDTIME

Five minutes, five minutes more, please!
  Let me stay five minutes more!
Can't I just finish the castle
  I'm building here on the floor?
Can't I just finish the story
  I'm reading here in my book?
Can't I just finish this bead-chain—
  It *almost* is finished, look!
Can't I just finish this game, please?
  When a game's once begun
It's a pity never to find out
  Whether you've lost or won.
Can't I just stay five minutes?
  Well, can't I stay just four?
Three minutes, then? two minutes?
  Can't I stay *one* minute more?

When cocks say Cockadoodledoo!
   The tree-top shakes,
   The river wakes,
And the daisy gets her eye of dew.

When the cuckoo says Cuckoo!
   The tree-top rustles,
   The river bustles,
The daisy's eye is wide to view.

When the wood–dove murmurs Croo!
   The tree-top shrinks,
   The river blinks,
The daisy hangs her head anew.

And when the brown owl calls Tu-whoo!
   The tree-top closes,
   The river dozes,
The daisy sleeps, and so must you.

A DRINK OF WATER

Mother has gone away. The night is black.
Whatever can I do to bring her back?
She tucked me in and kissed me once for all
And said good night, and told me not to call,
But oh, I want her so, I want her so!
What can I do to make her come? I know—
Mother! Mother! *Mo*-ther! (Listen! she's
Coming!) I want a drink of water, please.

27

Will she, when she comes to me, be vexed?
I don't care! I'll see her standing next
My bed, and hear her voice and touch her dress.
Will she, when she comes, I wonder, guess
I'm not *really* thirsty? *I* don't care!
I'll see her face again and smell her hair
As I sit up in bed upon my knees—   .
Mother! I want a drink of water, please.

She's come and gone. She held against my lips
The bedroom glass. I drank it in small sips
To make it last. She said, 'Don't call again,
Darling,' and smoothed the sheet and counterpane,
Kissed me, and went downstairs again. But oh,
I want her so, I want to see her so!
Mother! Mother! *Mo*-ther! *Mother!* (She's
Coming!) Another drink of water, please.

GOOD NIGHT

    Now good night.
Fold up your clothes
As you were taught,
Fold your two hands,
Fold up your thought;
Day is the plough-land,
Night is the stream,
Day is for doing
And night is for dream.
    Now good night.

LIGHT THE LAMPS UP, LAMPLIGHTER!

*For a Lamplighter, a Grandmother, The Angel Gabriel, and
Any Number of Others*

Light the lamps up, Lamplighter,
The people are in the street—
    Without a light
    They have no sight,
And where will they plant their feet?
Some will tread in the gutter,
And some in the mud—oh dear!
Light the lamps up, Lamplighter,
Because the night is here.

Light the candles, Grandmother,
The children are going to bed—
    Without a wick
    They'll stumble and stick,
And where will they lay their head?
Some will lie on the staircase,
And some in the hearth—oh dear!
Light the candles, Grandmother,
Because the night is here.

Light the stars up, Gabriel,
The cherubs are out to fly—
    If heaven is blind
    How will they find
Their way across the sky?
Some will splash in the Milky Way
Or bump on the moon—oh dear!
Light the stars up, Gabriel,
Because the night is here.

THE CRACK OF LIGHT

'No,' the little girl said,
As she snuggled down in bed,
'I don't have a night-light lit,
I'm not afraid a bit.

'But when you've got to go
Leave the door open *so*
With just a crack of light—
   Yes,' she said, '*that's* right!'

Down the stairs I went
And left her there content—
But oh, what happened then
She never told again.

She for her secret kept
What happened while she slept,
And hid what came at night
Through the crack of light.

GOING INTO DREAM

Where are you going, child, so far away?
Where you cannot follow to watch me at my play,
Light as a fallen feather floating on the stream
I'm going, going, back into the dream.

What will you find there, child, what will you do?
Something that I cannot ever tell to you,
Quiet as a moth flies across the candle-beam
I'm going, going back into the dream.

THE NIGHT WILL NEVER STAY

The night will never stay,
The night will still go by,
Though with a million stars
You pin it to the sky;
Though you bind it with the blowing wind
And buckle it with the moon,
The night will slip away
Like sorrow or a tune.

CHERRY STONES
AND
ROUND THE MULBERRY BUSH

How many cherries
Have you got?
Eat up your cherries
On the spot,
Count your cherry-stones,
Learn your lot,
Are you lucky
Or are you not?

SATIN

I had a satin slipper,
A single satin slipper
My mother left behind her
 The day she danced away.
So I stood on one toe,
Had to stand on one toe,
With the other toe behind me
 I just danced away.

I met the Lord of London,
The lofty Lord of London.
Before he fell behind me
 He knelt in my way.
 'One-foot-in-air-miss,
What about a pair, miss?
Cast a look behind you
 Before you dance away.'

I paired with him in satin,
Sheeny-shiny satin,
Seven yards behind me
    The train trailed away,
And my one satin slipper,
Glossy as a kipper.
I've never looked behind me
    From that day.

COTTON

My wedding-gown's cotton,
  My wedding-gown's cheap,
It's crisper than sea-foam
  And whiter than sheep,
Printed with daisies
  In yellow and green,
A prettier wedding-gown
  Never was seen!
Light-heart and light-foot
  I'll walk into church
As straight and as slim
  As a silvery birch,
And after my wedding
  I never will lay
Like ladies my wedding-gown
  Lightly away.

I'll wash it in soapsuds
  As fresh as when new,
And rinse it in rainwater
  Softer than dew,
And peg it on Saturdays
  High on the line,
And wear it on Sundays
  Full of sunshine.
My wedding-gown's cotton,
  It cost me a crown,
Was ever girl wed in
  A commoner gown?—
As birds in the branches,
  As flowers on the green,
The commonest wedding-gown
  Ever was seen!

TAILOR

I saw a little tailor sitting stitch, stitch, stitching
Cross-legged on the floor of his kitch, kitch, kitchen.
His thumbs and his fingers were so nim, nim, nimble
With his wax and his scissors and his thim, thim, thimble.
His silk and his cotton he was thread, thread, threading
For a gown and a coat for a wed, wed, wedding,
His needle flew as swift as a swal, swal, swallow,
And his spools and his reels had to fol, fol, follow.

He hummed as he worked a merry dit, dit, ditty:
'The bride is as plump as she's pret, pret, pretty,
I wouldn't have her taller or short, short, shorter,
She can laugh like the falling of wat, wat, water,

'She can put a cherry-pie, togeth, geth, gether,
She can dance as light as a feath, feath, feather,
She can sing as sweet as a fid, fid, fiddle,
And she's only twenty inches round the mid, mid,
  middle.'

The happy little tailor went on stitch, stitch, stitching
The black and the white in his kitch, kitch, kitchen.
He will wear the black one, she will wear the white one,
And the knot the parson ties will be a tight, tight, tight
  one.

SAILOR

My sweetheart's a sailor,
He sails on the sea,
When he comes home
He brings presents for me;
Coral from China,
Silks from Siam,
Parrots and pearls
From Seringatapam,
Silver from Mexico,
Gold from Peru,
Indian feathers
From Kalamazoo,
Scents from Sumatra,
Mantillas from Spain,
A fisherman's float
From the waters of Maine,
Reindeers from Lapland,
Ducks from Bombay,
A unicorn's horn
From the Land of Cathay—
Isn't it lucky
For someone like me
To marry a sailor
Who sails on the sea!

CARRIAGE

The Cream, the Bay,
The Dapple-Grey,
The Chestnut, and the Black,
Which will the Lady choose today
To trot her there and back?

The Cream can go
As soft as snow,
The Bay as fast as fire,
The Dapple-Grey is safe and slow
And never known to tire.

The Chestnut flies
As though the sky's
Gold chariot he drew,
The Black cavorts with flashing eyes
And nostrils bright with dew.

43

Oh in her fall
  Of lace and all
Her finery she goes
With loving hands from stall to stall,
As lovely as a rose.

  The Cream, the Bay,
  The Dapple-Grey,
The Chestnut, and the Black,
She's chosen all the five to-day
To bring her there and back.

WHEELBARROW

He dumped her in the wheelbarrow
  And trundled her away!
How he chaffed and how she laughed
  On their wedding day!

He bumped her through the garden-gate,
  He bounced her down the lane!
Then he reeled and then she squealed,
  And off they bounced again.

He jiggled her across the ditch,
  He joggled her through the holt!
He stubbed his toe and she cried O!
  Whenever she got a jolt.

He wiggled her up the bridle-path,
  He woggled her through the street—
Down he stumbled! down she tumbled,
  Right at the Parson's feet!

RICH MAN

I saw a Rich Man walking down the street
With a chain across his waistcoat and spats on his feet,
With silver in his pockets that jingled as he walked,
And a solid gold tooth that gleamed when he talked.
He walked by the girls with their baskets on their knees
Full of white clove pinks and pink sweet peas,
He walked by the flower-girls whose baskets smelled like
   honey
With his face full of care and his mind full of money.

I saw the Rich Man, he never saw me,
So I see more than the Rich Man can see.

POOR MAN

What have you got to eat,
                    poor man?
  Nothing, he said,
  But a crust of bread,
A crust that is shared is sweet,
                    poor man.

What sort of roof have you,
                    poor man?
  Nothing, he said
  But a shepherd's shed.
A shed that takes one takes two,
                    poor man.

What can you give your wife,
                    poor man?
  Nothing, he said,
  But hand, heart, and head.
It's a gift that will last for life,
                    poor man.

CASTLE

My castle is built in the air
    With turrets of light.
My husband is waiting up there
    Till I come in his sight.

It is built at the end of the day
    Of marble and gold
That always are melting away,
    So it never grows old.

Its gardens are crowded with rose
    And violet flowers,
Where the river of silver that flows
    Falls soon into showers

Sprinkling its shimmering stars
    On the vanishing green
Lawns. Then night puts up the bars,
    And the lawns lie unseen.

Each evening they build it anew,
    My castle up there,
Whose towers are the green and the blue
    And the gold of the air.

COTTAGE

When I live in a Cottage
I shall keep in my Cottage

Two different Dogs,
Three creamy Cows,
Four giddy Goats,
Five pewter Pots
Six silver Spoons
Seven busy Beehives
Eight ancient Appletrees
Nine red Rosebushes
Ten teeming Teapots
Eleven chirping Chickens
Twelve cosy Cats with their kittenish Kittens
     and
One blessèd Baby in a Basket.

That's what I'll have when I live in my Cottage.

Starling in my cherry-tree,
   It's *this* year!
I have counted three times three—
   It's *this* year!
P'raps before the next two cherries
   Make an earring
   For my wearing,
Or before the last bright berry's
   Come to sweeten
   And be eaten,
Or before the boughs are all in
   Yellow dresses
   Like princesses,
Or before the leaves have fallen,
   Light as butter—
   flies a-flutter—
         Listen, starling!
         Greedy darling,
Pecking in my cherry-tree,
   It's *this* year!
Peck your fill for all of me,
Since you left me three-times-three
For *this*-year, *this*-year, *this*-year, *this*-year,
         THIS-year!

NEVER

Never! wailed the wind.
Never! croaked the crow.
Never to be married,
   Oh, oh, oh!
What shall she do,
   Or where go?

Never! sobbed the star.
Never! moaned the moon.
Never to be married,
   Late or soon.
Not in January
   Or June.

Never! crowed the cock.
Never! clucked the hen.
Never to be married,
   Now or then.
Not one husband
   Among men.

Never! lisped the light.
Never! sighed the shade.
Never to be married,
   I'm afraid.
   Poor young maid!
   Poor Old Maid.

Follow your Leader
Wherever he goes!
Be at his heels
On the tips of your toes,
Echo the sounds he makes
All down the chain,
Mimic his gestures
How ever inane.
If he climbs you must climb,
If he crawls you must crawl,
Skip through the cellar,
And hop through the hall,
Cut through the kitchen
And stump up the stairs,
Dance round the dining-room

Table and chairs,
Barge through the bedrooms
And rumple the beds,
Leap up the ladder
That leads to the leads,
Grope in the gutters
And romp on the roof—
Then if your Leader
Demands a last proof,
And spreading his arms
Flies sky-high to the stars,
Follow your Leader
To Saturn or Mars.
But if he shouts 'Tea-time!'
Rush down in his wake
To brown bread-and-butter
And jam and plum-cake.

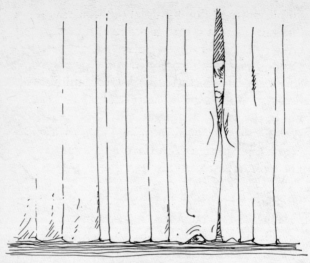

HIDE-AND-SEEK

Hiding

Tiptoe away! tiptoe away!
  While Jane is counting a hundred!
Where shall we go, above or below,
  While Jane is counting a hundred?
    Under the table?
      No, Mabel
        is there!
Behind the wings of the grandfather-chair?
  Hide in the curtain?
    I'm certain
        she'll see—
Creep away, creep away stealthily!

The linen-cupboard is warm and snug—
Peter's wrapped up in the travelling rug.

Don't whisper! don't giggle! *sh!* look alive—
I'm sure she has got to forty-five!
Under the bed is a lovely place—
Oh bother, it's full of Gwen and Grace.
The wardrobe is stuffed with Dick and Kate—
I'm certain she's got to sixty-eight!
Up to the attics do a bunk,
Perhaps there's room in the wooden trunk—
No, it is crammed with Caroline.
She *must* have got to Seventy-nine!

Hide here! hide there! hide anywhere,
    While Jane is counting a hundred!
        Be quick! be quiet! oh, do play fair
    While Jane is counting a hundred!
        Hold your breath!
        Stand still as death!
Squeeze up, Roger, make room for Beth!
        Don't push!
                don't rush!

    She is coming—hush!
She has finished counting her hundred!

Seeking

When little Jane lifts up her head,
    Uncovering her eyes,
Every other child has fled
    Into the mysteries.
The playmates that she knew are gone,
    And Jane is left alone.

Oh Alice with the starry looks,
    Oh Ann with gleaming curls,
What dusky corners, what dim nooks
    Have hid you little girls?
The house is vast and Jane is small,
    And are you here at all?

Oh Richard with the flashing smile,
    Oh Rob with freckled brow,
Where are you hiding all this while,
    You who were here but now?
The house lies in a sleep as deep
    As Sleeping Beauty's sleep.

Through all the rooms grown deaf and blind
    Jane seeks with throbbing heart
The hidden playmates whom to find
    Will make small tremors start—
For when she finds them in the game.
    They may not be the same.

A thimble, a thimble! my Mother's gold thimble
  Is somewhere in sight if it's true what we're told.
Blue, brown and hazel eyes, spying and prying,
  Are hunting my Mother's wee thimble of gold.

As soon as your nimble glance lights on the thimble,
  Sit down very softly and don't turn a hair.
One after other sits down, while my Mother
  Rocks backwards and forwards and smiles in her chair.

Is it perched on a picture, or propped on a statue,
  Or stuck in the keyhole instead of the key?
Oh thimble, perhaps I am looking right *at* you!
  Is *that* you? Is *that* you? Oh, where can you be?

Perhaps on the piano—the inkstand—the fender—
  Or on the brass coal-scuttle gleaming so bright?
They all have sat down! Shall I have to surrender?
  The little gold thimble is nowhere in sight.

A thimble, a thimble, my Mother's wee thimble!—
  But why as she rocks is she laughing at me?
You booby! just linger to look on my finger—
  Where else do you think that a thimble should be?

TOUCH

He! He! He!
He's after you and me!
Run! for his lightest touch
Will alter us so much.

His fingertip may change
   The shapes we live within
To forms with spirits strange
   And creatures queer of skin

You might become a snake,
   I might become a swan,
Tomorrow you might wake
   Up a Mastadon,

Or I might be a mole,
   Or you a waterfall,
Or I a fiery coal,
   Or both not here at all!

He! He! He!
He's after you and me!
Oh run from him! His touch
Would alter us too much.

Oranges and Lemons

Oranges bright as the sun!
Lemons as pale as the moon!
Here they come, one after one,
All to be harvested soon.
Under the arch they go flinging,
Bursting with laughter and singing
With all the town bell-ringers ringing and swinging their
tune.

Candles and bed-time are near—
Look! we have caught you, my dear,
Now whisper low in my ear
Which one will *you* be, which one?
A lemon as pale as the moon and as clear,
Or an orange as bright as the sun?
Don't let the other ones hear!

Now once again they go swinging,
Swinging and springing along,
And all the town steeples are ringing and flinging and
singing their song!

BLIND MAN'S BUFF

Blindman! Blindman! Blundering about,
Barging round the furniture with hands stretched out.
Bind his eyes and blind his eyes with thick dark stuff,
Mind you see the handkerchief is tied tight enough!

Buffet the old buffer! Biff him in the back!
Tug him by the coat-tails, turn him off his track,
Twist and tease and tickle him, tweak him by the cuff,
Baffle the old buffer in Blind Man's Buff!

Ha, ha, Blindman! snatching at the air!
Ho, ho, Blindman! catching at a chair!
He, he, Blindman! clutching at *me*—
Ha, ha! ho, ho! he, he, he!

    Bustle him and hustle him,
    Muddle and befuddle him,
Bang him off his balance—don't be a funk!
    Banter him! befoozle him!
    Bewilder him! bamboozle him!
Batter, bait, and badger him, and then do a bunk!

Blindman! Blindman! See how he spins!
Bumping and stumping and barking of his shins!
Rumple him and crumple him, treat the buffer rough—
But beware if he should bag you in Blind Man's Buff!

HERE WE GO
ROUND THE MULBERRY BUSH

There is a bush that no one sees,
The loveliest of little trees,
Full of sweet dark mulberries.

Round and round it children go,
Sometimes quick and sometimes slow,
Singing words all children know.

While they sing the bush is there
Planted in the empty air,
With fruit for every child to share,

Little girls with sandalled foot,
Little boys in clumping boot,
Running round the mulberry root,

Fair and dark ones, loitering, leaping,
Gay and grave ones, laughing, weeping,
Playing, working, waking, sleeping.

When the moment's game is done,
When the playing child is gone,
The unseen mulberry bush stands on,

And with all its leafy eyes
Childhood's flickering shadow spies
Dancing down the centuries,

And with all its leafy ears
Evermore the footstep hears
Of vanished childhood's hundred years,

Singing still without a sound,
Running silently around
The bush that never grew in ground.

OLD AND YOUNG

Rockaby, my baby,
Slumber if you can.
I wonder what you're going to be
When you're grown a man.

If you are a monarch
On a gold and silver throne,
With all the lands of East and West
For to call your own,
I know you'll be the greatest monarch
Ever was known.

If you are a poet
With the magic of the word,
A swan's quill to write with
And a voice like a bird,
I know you'll be the greatest poet
Ever was heard.

But whether you're a monarch
And make your bride a queen,
Or whether you're a poet
With men's hearts to glean,
I know you are the sweetest baby
Ever was seen.

Rockaby, my baby,
Slumber if you can.
I wonder what you're going to be
When you're grown a man.

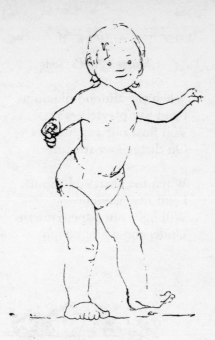

BABY STANDS

Look! my baby's standing there
With her hands upon the chair.
Suddenly she lifts her hands,
And one wondrous moment stands

Bright-eyed, flushed, surprised and sweet,
On her two unsteady feet.

Down she goes, then—down she goes!
Oh, but how she laughs and crows,

Laughs and crows as though to say,
She *did* take her hands away!

71

WHEN THE ALMOND BLOSSOMS

Chinese Child's Song

When the almond blossoms,
I and my playfellows
Will float our paper boats
On the yellow stream.

When the cherry blossoms,
I and my playfellows
Will light our paper lanterns
Under the white bough.

GIRLS' NAMES

What lovely names for girls there are!
There's Stella like the Evening Star,
And Sylvia like a rustling tree,
And Lola like a melody,
And Flora like a flowery morn,
And Sheila like a field of corn,
And Melusina like the moan
Of water. And there's Joan, like Joan.

BOYS' NAMES

What splendid names for boys there are!
There's Carol like a rolling car,
And Martin like a flying bird,
And Adam like the Lord's First Word,
And Raymond like the Harvest Moon,
And Peter like a piper's tune,
And Alan like the flowing on
Of water. And there's John, like John.

DAVID

Yes, David puts his toys away,
And washes behind his ears,
     If he climbs a tree
     And scrapes his knee
He doesn't resort to tears;
He never gives girls and boys away,
He has the politest tones,
In fact, he is a *good* little boy,
But he *will—throw—stones*.

He throws them at the window-panes,
He throws them at the water,
He throws them at his Aunty Jane's
Inoffensive daughter,
He throws them for old Rover to
Bring back again like treasure,
He throws them Over, At, and Through,
For nothing else but pleasure;
He shies at acorns, conkers, cones,
And always scores a single,
He chucks his stones at other stones
Lying on the shingle,
He aims at stumps and sitting hens,
He marks down running rabbits—
It's just another of you men's
Incalculable habits.
He has no motive deep and dark,
That isn't it a bit, it
Is: that when David spies his mark
He *simply—has*—to hit it.

David gives his things away,
And brushes his teeth at night,
  He seldom fails
  To clean his nails,
And get his homework right,
And everybody brings away
The same report with groans:
'David *is* a good little boy,
But he *does—throw—stones*!'

CLARE

When I'm grown up, *thought black-haired Clare*,
I'm going to have waved golden hair
    And dress in lupin-blue,
And on my desk a very thin
Green glassy vase with roses in,
    Never more than two

I'll wear a curious kind of ring,
And let a lump of amber swing
    Upon a silver chain
Around my neck, like honey spun,
  No, rather like a spot of sun
    Hung on drops of rain.
When I speak, my voice will be
Something like the sound of sea
    On shingle, sort of hoarse
With clearer ripples in between,
Murmury and low, I mean,
    And heavenly, of course.
My hat will have a darling brim,
Not the sort of hat you trim
    With flowers and ribbons much,
But *fascinating*, and my hand
Will seem to love and understand
    Whatever it may touch.
And when I stand upright, it will
Be like a birch-tree, not quite still
    But just about to dance;
And where I move, a very light
Sweet scent will float, like stocks at night
    In a sort of trance . . .

Oh Clare, my child! *Miss Wilson, gowned*
In lupin-blue, Miss Wilson, crowned
  With shining waves of gold,
Miss Wilson with the murmuring tones
Like water lapping on salt stones,
  But now so cold, so cold—
  Oh Clare, my child! *the cold voice spoke*
  Your work is something past a joke.

  If only you could love
And concentrate on something! *said*
Miss Wilson. Clare, where *is* your head?
  What *are* you dreaming of?

PETER

It's all very well, said Peter to Mike,
To say Be brave! but how would you like
When the water runs out with a *glug-glug-glug,*
How would *you* like to be sucked down the Plug?

Next year, when I am as big as you,
I'll sit it out to the finish too,
See if I don't! and let it run
Away till the very last drop is done.

And the squelchy sound it makes in the hole
Won't bother me then, upon my soul!
But this year it's all very well to sneer—
Just you remember yourself last year.

You've *forgot* how the hole gets bigger and bigger
Till it's bigger around than your own figure!
It's so long ago, you've *forgot* what it's like,
That's what it is, said Peter to Mike.

And I *will* get out when the water goes *glug!*
And I *won't* be sucked down the Bathroom Plug!

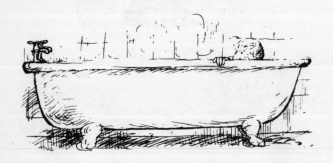

GRISELDA

Griselda is greedy, I'm sorry to say.
She isn't contented with four meals a day,
Like breakfast and dinner and supper and tea
(I've had to put tea after supper—you see
          Why, don't you?)
Griselda is greedy as greedy can be.

She snoops about the larder
For sundry small supplies,
She breaks the little crusty bits
Off rims of apple pies,
She pokes the roast-potato-dish
When Sunday dinner's done,
And if there are two left in it
Griselda snitches one;
Cold chicken and cold cauliflower
She pulls in little chunks—
And when Cook calls:
          'What are you doing there?'
              Griselda bunks.

79

Griselda is greedy. Well, that's how she feels,
She simply can't help eating in-between meals,
And always forgets what it's leading to, though
The Doctor has frequently told her: 'You know
               Why, *don't* you?'
When the stomach-ache starts and Griselda says:
    'Oh.'

      She slips down to the dining-room
      When everyone's in bed,
      For cheese-rind on the supper-tray,
      And buttered crusts of bread,
      A biscuit from the biscuit-box,
      Lump sugar from the bowl,
      A gherkin from the pickle-jar,
      Are all Griselda's toll;
      She tastes the salted almonds,
      And she tries the candied fruits—
And when Dad shouts:
      'Who *is* it down below?'
      Griselda scoots.

Griselda is greedy. Her relatives scold,
And tell her how sorry she'll be when she's old,
She will lose her complexion, she's sure to grow fat,
She will spoil her inside—does she know what she's at?
          (Why *do* they?)
Some people *are* greedy. Leave it at that.

NED

It's a singular thing that Ned
Can't be got out of bed.
    When the sun comes round
    He is sleeping sound
With the blankets over his head.
    They tell him to shunt,
    And he gives a grunt,
And burrows a little deeper—
    He's a trial to them
    At eight am,
When Ned is a non-stop sleeper.

Oh, the snuggly bits
Where the pillow fits
Into his cheek and neck!
Oh, the beautiful heat
Stored under the sheet
Which the breakfast-bell will wreck!
Oo, the snoozly-oozly feel
He feels from head to heel,
When to get out of bed
Is worse to Ned
Than missing his morning meal!
But
It's a singular thing that Ned,
After the sun is dead
And the moon's come round,
Is not to be found,
And can't be got into bed!

In goes Robin, bold as brass,
Into all that moving mass
Of blue and green and creamy foam
Just as though he were at home.
Water doesn't frighten him,
He will sink till he can swim,
When a big wave knocks him down
Up will come his laughing brown
Spluttering face. He has no fear,
The sea is his: yes, all that clear
Stretch of water, touching all
The shores of earth, that makes its call
On English cliffs and Indian sands,
And coral isles and mountain-lands,
And crowded ports and lonely bays:
His, should he choose to go those ways,
With all the ships that sail on it,
And all the gulls and mews that flit,
And all the fishes in the blue,
And all the wrecks and icebergs too.
The sea was Robin's from the first,
He saw it and was all athirst,
He couldn't *wait* to reach it—whether
Its waves were tumbled all together,
Or it was bright and smooth as glass,
In went Robin, bold as brass.

IN MY YOUNG DAY

'It were all fields in my young day,
Green fields and flowers,' the old man said.
'My father kep' a stack o' hay
Here where the Garridge stands. We fed
Our goat on it. I hears him bleat
Yet, the old goat, and sees him butt.
The meadow-grass it smelled that sweet!
Now it's all petrol and black smut.

'It were the rarest field for oaks
To climb in hereabouts, you know.
Them fact'ry-chimbleys (how they smokes!)
Must be a long sight taller, though.
Where yonder flats are, you'd ha' seen
A pond! That field 'ud take a prize
For buttercups in June—and green!
Lord, what a sight for weary eyes!'

'Don't you mind him, sir,' said the smart
Young chauffeur. 'We just let him talk.
Things have looked up some in this part
Since *his* time. Where men had to walk
Then, they ride now. That's progress, eh?
Green fields, my oath! I couldn't stick
His fields! At eight, sir, did you say?
Right-O! I'll be there on the tick.'

THE BEGGAR

A beggar with a ragged jacket,
  And battered hat upon his head,
And matches in a little packet,
  Stood on the kerb, and nothing said.
He did not even raise his eye
As on my business I went by.

If he had asked, I might have hurried;
  If he had looked, I might have fled;
But just because he never worried,
  And stood quite still, and nothing said,
I found I could not pass him by.
I gave, and he took, silently.

Eliza Ottley, seventy-five,
In Windsor all her life did thrive.
Her father once had mended chairs
And woven baskets for the wares
Of livelihood. When he was dead
Eliza also earned her bread
By plaiting rush and weaving cane.
No poor one asked her alms in vain,
Her only penny she would give
That others, like herself, might live,
For the big cloak she wore kept warm
Her ageless heart and ageing form.
She dwelt alone, but loved the words
And ways of children and of birds—
Much lore she read by hook or crook,
And Shakespeare was her favourite book—
So, rich in nature, poor in wealth,
She reached old age in perfect health.

One day when it was wet and wild,
She met a poor soul with a child.
Swift her big cloak she had undone
To wrap around the little one,
And, getting wet, at last took cold,
Died, and was given to the mould.

This is the tale of one plain life.
Never a mother or a wife,
Eliza Ottley, seventy-five,
Died that another's child might live
Mother of Jesus, lay your blue
Cloak round her when she comes to you.

Here hangs a garland
On a cleft stick,
The four winds of heaven
Round it are met;
When time has withered
The flower that was quick,
The four winds of heaven
Shall sing of it yet:
 Windyfield! Windyfield!
 Never forget.

Here dwells a woman,
Agatha Blyth,
The four winds of heaven
Blow round her cot,
When time has reaped her,
A flower for his scythe,
The four winds of heaven
Shall sing on the spot:
 Agatha! Agatha!
 Never forget.

AT A WINDOW

At an open window
In a small white house
I saw a little bent head
Quiet as a mouse;
A cap of snow-white linen
Covered all its hair—
I thought it was a baby
Sitting up there.

The little figure turned
Its face, so white to see;
It was an old, old woman
Looking out on me.
Ninety were the years
That had worn her white and spare—
I must have seemed a young thing
Standing down there.

I looked up.
She looked down.
Then she raised a thin white arm
Over her white crown,
And waved very softly
Her hand in the air
Like a welcome and a leave-taking
To me out there.

Grandfather Penny
Of Euston is dead.
Untended of any
He died in his bed.
He died without mother
Or sister or brother,
It's whispered by many
He died without bread.

But the children that knew him,
Who play in the streets,
Would always run to him
To get penny treats.
When bread put its price on,
He never thought twice on
The gift of a penny
For poor children's sweets.

Grandfather Penny,
Old, gentle, and thin,
There will not be many
Who heaven will win,
Whose penny rings sweeter
In ear of Saint Peter,
When he opens the gate,
And says, 'Granfer, come in.'

AROUND THE YEAR

A ROUND FOR THE NEW YEAR

Round the ring around
Take each other's hands!
He who pauses in the round
Falls out where he stands.

Take each other's hands
Round around the ring—
Here we stand in winter-time,
Soon we'll stand in spring.

Round around the ring
As we go about,
Old Year pauses where he stands—
Old Year, fall you out!

As we go about
The ground begins to spin—
New Year can the fastest run,
New Year, come you in!

The ground begins to spin,
Spin with the ground,
Take each other's hands again,
Round the ring around!

THREE MILES TO PENN

Today I walked three miles to Penn
With an uneasy mind.
The sun shone like a frozen eye,
A light that had gone blind.
The glassy air between the sky
And earth was frozen wind—
All motion and all light again
Were closed within a rind,
As I by wood and field to Penn
Took trouble in my mind.

The slopes of cloud in heaven that lay,
Unpeopled hills grown old,
Had no more movement than the land
Locked in a flowing mould;
The sheep like mounds of cloudy sand
Stood soundless in the cold;
There was no stir on all the way
Save what my heart did hold,
So quiet earth and heaven lay,
So quiet and so old.

By Dippel Woods

I knew no woman, child, or man
Had been before my steps today.
By Dippel Woods the snow-lanes ran
Soft and uncrushed above their clay;
But little starry feet had traced
Their passages as though in words,
And all those lanes of snow were laced
With runnings of departed birds.

Child, take your basket down,
Go and find spring,
Earth has not lost her brown,
Nor wind his sting,
But in the morning
The thrush and the blackbird
Sing to the sleeping town,
And to the waking woods
Sing:
     take your basket down,
Go and find spring!

Now where the ground was bare
Only last week,
Now where the flower was rare
And the hedge bleak,
Reach for the catkin
And stoop for the primrose,
Seek, if you want your share
Of the first gathering,
Seek,
     where the ground was bare
Only last week.

HOUSE HUNTERS

Birds will be house-hunting
  Soon—think of that!
Crows in the elm-tops
  And larks on the flat,
Owls in the belfry
  And wrens in the leaves,
And swifts will go house-hunting
  Under the eaves.

Moorhen will hunt for her
   House in the reeds,
Chaffinch the apple-tree
   Bough ere she breeds,
Thrush in the hollow oak,
   Sparrow won't care—
Here, there, and everywhere,
   Any old where!

Cuckoo won't trouble,
   She'll just stop and call,
But starling and nightingale,
   Blackbird and all,
Jays as they chatter,
   And doves as they croon,
Soon will be house-hunting,
   Think of it—soon!

BROKEN WING

We found a little bird in spring
   New-fallen from its nest,
It had a pretty broken wing
   And a small hurt on its breast.

We took it home and laid it soft
   In flannel and green grass,
The milk and crumbs we brought it oft
   It could not eat, alas!

It was too young to pipe aloud,
   It was too hurt to fly,
And grass and flannel were its shroud
   When it came to die.

PANCAKE TUESDAY

Run to Church with a Frying-Pan!
A Kiss for the Woman, a Cake for the Man.

Run to Church with a frying-pan,
  Never you lose a minute!
Run to Church with a frying-pan
  And a yellow pancake in it.

First to carry her pancake there,
  Though heavy or light she beat it,
Must toss her cake to the Bellringer,
  And the Bellringer must eat it.
Then be she madam or be she miss
  All breathless after rushing,
The Bellringer shall give her his kiss
  And never mind her blushing.

A Kiss for the Woman, a Cake for the Man—
Run to Church with a Frying-Pan!

A MORNING SONG

For the First Day of Spring

Morning has broken
Like the first morning,
Blackbird has spoken
 Like the first bird.
Praise for the singing!
Praise for the morning!
Praise for them, springing
 From the first Word.

103

Sweet the rain's new fall
Sunlit from heaven,
Like the first dewfall
    In the first hour.
Praise for the sweetness
Of the wet garden,
Sprung in completeness
    From the first shower.

Mine is the sunlight!
Mine is the morning
Born of the one light
    Eden saw play.
Praise with elation,
Praise every morning
Spring's re-creation
    Of the First Day!

THE CUCKOO COMES

This is the day
When cuckoos sing,
And people say
Here comes Spring.
But wise birds stay
With guarding breasts
On Cuckoo-day
To save their nests.

FOR EASTER

On Easter Day in the Morning the Door of Heaven
  stands wide,
On Easter Day in the Morning the Angels wait outside,
The Angels in their Garments with Sheaves of Silver
  Palms
They wait till Love rise up from Earth to beg for Heaven's
  Alms.
      On Easter Day in the Morning,
      On Easter Day in the Morning,
On Easter Day in the Morning Love shall rise again,
He shall come to the Door of Heaven and beg a Boon for
  Men.

FOR A DANCE

Round the Maypole dance about,
Dance your Ribbons in and out;
When they're plaited, then begin
To dance your Ribbons out and in.
Green and Yellow this way, that way Red and Blue,
Plait the Dance, unplait the Dance, and plait the Dance
anew!

They called my buttercup a weed
And told me, 'Pull it up!'
I let it stand and flower and seed,
My golden buttercup.

Next year when it was twice its size,
'Root out that weed!' they said.
I let it stand and spread and rise
And seed upon its bed.

In the third year when it came up
My gold-weed was a bower,
And when they saw my buttercup,
They cried out, '*What* a flower!'

Down the street the old man came,
And on his head he bore a flame.

I stopped to gaze, so he stopped too.
'Want some?' he said. 'Indeed I do.

Where did you get them?' 'Uxbridge way,
All the lot fresh-picked today

Off the island there,' he said,
Shifting the basket from his head.

'You gets 'em when the water's out,
O' course. I had to wait about

All night for 'em. The bud'll bloom
Lovely when they're in your room.'

I took the bunch from him, still wet,
And then the kingcup-gatherer set

His brimming basket on his old
Grey head, and walked beneath the gold,

Yes, walked off in his broken boots,
And the shabbiest of suits,

Crowned in the may-time of the spring,
More gloriously than a king.

SAINT SWITHIN'S WISH

16th July

I'll lie (said Swithin)
Somewhere within
Sound of things
Like birds' wings,
Raindrops' beat,
Insects' feet,
Cows lowing,
Peasants going,
Seeds springing,
People singing,
Boys clattering,
Girls chattering,
Men walking,
Women talking,
Children's tread
  (Swithin said).
Who shifts the earth wherein I lie
For forty days shall not go dry.

WHO'S THAT BLEATING?

Who's that bleating
Down by river?
Sheep are sweating,
Soon they'll shiver.
Back to farm
Without their wool,
We'll go warm
And they'll go cool.

111

All the way to Alfriston,
From Chichester to Alfriston,
I went along the running Downs
High above the patchwork plain,
Fantastical as Joseph's coat
With coloured squares of grass and grain,
Earthen russets, duns, and browns,
Charlock-yellow, clover-green,
Reddening wheat and silvery oat:
And rivers coiling in between,
And roofs of little peopled towns.

I heard the wind among the leaves
And corn that was not yet in sheaves
Swishing with the sound of surf;
I heard the cry of distant trains,
The rush and drip of scudding rains,
I heard my foot-beat on the turf,
The lark's delight, the pewit's plaint,
Hoarse calls of shepherds, bark and bleat,
Sheep-bells and church-bells in the heat,
And rambling thunders, far and faint:
And I saw dew-ponds round as pearls,
And multitudes of summer flowers,
Mulleins tall as little girls,

And Canterbury Bells in showers,
Fields flushed with sainfoin, banks that blazed
With golden toad-flax and such fires
Of poppy that I was amazed;
And chicory as blue as heaven
Seen in clear water: I saw spires,
And thatches, castles, barns, and towers,
The furnace of a clinking forge
And bridges made of wood and stone;
And by an ancient hostel even
Saw demons in the open street,
A rabbit at a Bishop's feet,
Angels and dragons and Saint George,
When I was come to Alfriston.

I ate my bread on open places,
I changed a smile with many faces,
I loved the jokes and commerce with
The jolly baker and the smith,
The gypsy with her wheedling eyes,
Her pack of wares, her pack of lies;
I loved the rain-storms and the sun,
The silent shepherds young and old,
I loved the cropping, wandering fold,
The silky dog that chased the sheep,
I loved my rest when day was done,
I loved the Downs, awake, asleep,
All the way to Alfriston,
From Chichester to Alfriston.

THE CHILD IN THE TRAIN

The train stands still
  And the world runs by.
Yonder runs a tree
  And a cloud in the sky.
Here flies a pony
  On the running road,
And there flows the quickest
  River ever flowed.

115

The mountains on the edge
    Roll away like the tide,
The backs of the houses,
    Pass on a slide,
The little farms slip off
    As soon as one looks,
And the little churches vanish
    With their spires and their rooks.

The buttercup embankments,
    The telegraph wires,
The names of the stations,
    The small heath fires,
The hoardings in the fields,
    And the people in the street,
Go whizzing into somewhere
    While I keep my seat.

The little cities trot,
    And the little hamlets trip,
The meadow with its cow,
    The sea with its ship,
The forest and the factory,
    The hedge and the hill—
The world goes running by
    While the train stands still!

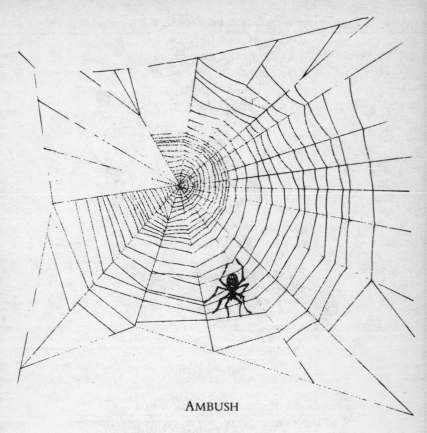

AMBUSH

The spider in its web of grey
Scarce visible in brightest day,
Now lurks in ambush, like a spy,
To catch the unsuspicious fly.

To soon, too soon the gauzy wings
Of fragile sun-delighting things
Destroyed in Autumn's shroud will lie
Woven to catch the summer fly.

THE BONFIRE

This cloud of smoke in other hours
Was leaves and grass, green twigs and flowers.

This bitter-sweet dead smell that blows
Was once the breathing of the rose.

Shapeless the forms of petals fair
And slender leaves melt on the air,

And in a scent she never knew
In life, the rose departeth too.

HELTERY-SKELTERY

Run, rabbit, run!
Run to your warren
The harvest is done,
The meadow is barren,
The corn was your shelter
From stone, stick, and gun,
Heltery-skeltery
Run, rabbit, run!

THE PLOUGHBOY

If I was a Ploughboy and followed the plough,
  All over the earth with my plough I would go,
My horse would plod patiently up to the brow
  And patiently plod to the valley below.

Wherever he plodded the furrows would go
  On the face of the land like the rays of the sun,
On black field and brown field they'd lie in a row
  And close on the heels of my ploughing they'd run.

I'd walk by my horse till my ploughing was done,
  Or sit on a shaft, swing my feet, and say Ho!
I'd munch bread and cheese when the church clock struck
  one!
  And wait for the summer to see the things grow.

THIS BREAD

This bread,
This bread
That carelessly you crumble,
Was once the red
Wheat, the green oat, the humble
Barley that filled
The dreams of the unfed,
Man, woman, and child.
Respect this holy bread.

BROTHERS AND SISTERS

4th October, St Francis's Day

Come forth, O beasts! This is the day
　Of that dear Saint who called you brother,
Who greeted you upon the way
　As one companion does another,
And saw in God's creative plan
No difference between beast and man.

Fly down, O birds! This is the day
　Of that sweet Saint who sister named you,
Who, coming in your midst to pray,
　By love, and by love only, tamed you,
And read in the Creator's word
Equal delight for man and bird.

What! not one furry thing runs out?
　What! not a single flying feather?
Men separate with fear and doubt
　What love was wont to bring together.
To bird and beast we call in vain
Till Brother Francis walks again.

NOW! Says Time,
and lifts his finger,
and the leaf on the lime
may not linger.
When Time utters
NOW! and lifts
his finger, the oakleaf flutters
and drifts,
and elm and beech
let a leaf fall from the bough
when, finger lifted, to each
Time says NOW!

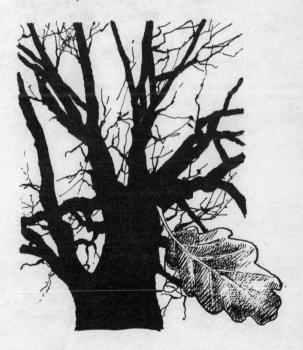

MYFANWY AMONG THE LEAVES

Dying leaf and dead leaf,
Yellow leaf and red leaf
And white-backed beam,
Lay along the woodland road
As quiet as a dream.

Summer was over,
The year had lost her lover,
Spent with her grief
All along the woodland road
Leaf fell on leaf.

Then came a shuffling,
Such a happy ruffling
Of the dried sweet
Surf of leaves upon the road
Round a baby's feet.

Year-old leaf ran after
Three-year-old laughter,
Danced through the air
As she caught them from the road
And flung them anywhere.

Old leaf and cold leaf,
Brown leaf and gold leaf
And white-backed beam,
Followed down the woodland road
Myfanwy in a dream.

The Old Man sweeps the leaves
Fallen everywhere
Through the soft cool air.
Each shake of wind bereaves
Some bough, and leaves it bare.

The gutters of old eaves
Are clogged with them, the feet
Of passers in the street
Shuffle the rustling sheaves
To chatter shrill and sweet.

The earth her own receives,
The layered hordes have flowed
Thick on the woodland road,
And time the burden weaves
Into one matted load.

And children go to school,
And none of them believes
In the bare tree, or grieves
To see how in the cool
The Old Man sweeps the leaves.

'PUNKIE-NIGHT'

A Somersetshire Custom on 30th October

Here come children
On Punkie-night
With mangold-lanterns,
And candle-light
Gleaming inside
The goblin-faces'
Yellowy grins
And gold grimaces.
In and out
Of Hinton St George,
By church and hostel,
By farm and forge,
Swinging their gargoyle
Mangolds bright,
There go children
On Punkie-night.

Wind bloweth,
Water floweth
Feather flieth,
Bird goeth.
Whither, bird?
Who can tell?
None knoweth . . .
Farewell.

Wind bawleth,
Summer palleth,
Rose fadeth,
Leaf falleth.
Wither, leaf.
Where you fell,
Winter calleth . . .
Farewell.

Tree turneth,
Bonfire burneth,
Earth resteth,
Sleep earneth.
Whither, earth?
To dream a spell
Till flower returneth . . .
Sleep well.

On Hallowe'en the old ghosts come
About us, and they speak to some;
To others they are dumb.

They haunt the hearts that loved them best;
In some they are by grief possessed,
In other hearts they rest.

They have a knowledge they would tell;
To some of us it is a knell,
To some a miracle.

They come unseen and go unseen;
And some will never know they've been,
And some know all they mean.

PENCIL AND PAINT

Winter has a pencil
For pictures clear and neat,
She traces the black tree-tops
Upon a snowy sheet.
But autumn has a palette
And a painting-brush instead,
And daubs the leaves for pleasure
With yellow, brown, and red.

ROBIN TO JENNY

The frost is on the ground, Jenny,
    Too hard for bill to crack,
And where shall food be found, Jenny,
    That you and I now lack?
Oh thanks be to the burrowing mole
    That still throws up his hill—
His fresh-turned earth's my goal, Jenny,
    And that will feed us still.

The ground is like a rock, Jenny,
    A rock I cannot break!
Poor Robin can't unlock, Jenny,
    It's larder for your sake;
So thanks be to the working-man
    That doth his garden till—
We from his furrow can, Jenny,
    Get that will feed us still.

The ground is hard as ice, Jenny,
    Of every comfort bare,
And where shall I look twice, Jenny,
    To get your daily fare?
Now thanks be to the girl or boy
    That strews the window-sill—
Come spring we'll sing them joy, Jenny,
    Because they fed us still.

When trees did show ño leaves,
   And grass no daisies had,
And fields had lost their sheaves,
   And streams in ice were clad,
And day of light was shorn,
   And wind had got a spear,
Jesus Christ was born
   In the ending of the year.

Like green leaves when they grow,
   He shall for comfort be;
Like life in streams shall flow,
   For running water He;
He shall raise hope like corn
   For barren fields to bear,
And therefore He was born
   In the ending of the year.

Like daisies to the grass,
   His innocence He'll bring;
In keenest winds that pass
   His flowering love shall spring;
The rising of the morn
   At midnight shall appear,
Whenever Christ is born
   In the ending of the year.

WHEN CHRISTMAS COMES

This is the week when Christmas comes,
  Let every pudding burst with plums,
And every tree bear dolls and drums,
  In the week when Christmas comes.

Let every hall have boughs of green,
With berries glowing in between,
  In the week when Christmas comes.

Let every doorstep have a song
Sounding the dark street along,
  In the week when Christmas comes.

Let every steeple ring a bell
With a joyful tale to tell,
  In the week when Christmas comes.

Let every night put forth a star
To show us where the heavens are,
  In the week when Christmas comes.

Let every pen enfold a lamb
Sleeping warm beside its dam,
  In the week when Christmas comes.

This is the week when Christmas comes.

THE CHILDREN'S CAROL

Here we come again, again, and here we come again!
Christmas is a single pearl swinging on a chain,
Christmas is a single flower in a barren wood,
Christmas is a single sail on the salty flood,
Christmas is a single star in the empty sky,
Christmas is a single song sung for charity.
Here we come again, again, to sing to you again,
Give a single penny that we may not sing in vain.

My Baby, my Burden,
   Tomorrow the morn
I shall go lighter
   And you will be born.

I shall go lighter,
   But heavier too,
For seeing the burden,
   That falls upon you.

The burden of love,
   The burden of pain,
I'll see you bear both
   Among men once again.

Tomorrow you'll bear it
   Your burden alone,
Tonight you've no burden
   That is not my own.

My Baby, my Burden,
   Tomorrow the morn
I shall go lighter
   And you will be born.

SAINT NICHOLAS

Nicholas, Saint of Children,
Loves to spend his wealth
On pretty toys for girls and boys,
Leaving them by stealth.
The wind in the chimney
Hears children call:
'Bring me this, Saint Nicholas!
Bring me that, Saint Nicholas!
    A silky scarf,
    A bag of sweets,
    A big gold ball!'

Nicholas, Saint of Sailors,
Children of the sea,
When their sails are torn by gales
Close at hand is he.
The wind in the rigging
Hears the sailors cry:
'Save us here, old Nicholas!
Save us there, good Nicholas!
    Saint of Sailors,
    Bring us safe
    Home, high and dry!'

CRADLE SONG FOR CHRISTMAS

Child, when on this night you lie
Softly, undisturbedly,
On as white a bed of down
As any child's in London Town,
By a fire that all the night
Keeps your bedroom warm and light:
Dreams, if dreams are yet your law,
Your bed of down a bed of straw,
Only warmed and lighted by
One star in the open sky.
Sweet you'll sleep then, for we know
Once a Child slept sweetly so.

THIS HOLY NIGHT

God bless your house this holy night,
   And all within it;

God bless the candle that you light
   To midnight's minute:

The board at which you break your bread,
   The cup you drink of:

And as you raise it, the unsaid
   Name that you think of:

The warming fire, the bed of rest,
   The ringing laughter:

These things, and all things else be blest
   From floor to rafter

This holy night, from dark to light,
   Even more than other;

And, if you have no house tonight,
   God bless you, brother.

NOW EVERY CHILD

Now every Child that dwells on earth,
  Stand up, stand up and sing!
The passing night has given birth
  Unto the Children's King.
    Sing sweet as the flute,
      Sing clear as the horn,
    Sing joy of the Children
      Come Christmas the morn!
    Little Christ Jesus
      Our Brother is born.

Now every Star that dwells in sky,
  Look down with shining eyes!
The night has dropped in passing by
  A Star from Paradise.
    Sing sweet as the flute,
      Sing clear as the horn,
    Sing joy of the Stars
      Come Christmas the morn!
    Little Christ Jesus
      Our Brother is born.

Now every Beast that crops in field,
  Breathe sweetly and adore!
The night has brought the richest yield
  That ever harvest bore.
    Sing sweet as the flute,
      Sing clear as the horn,
    Sing joy of the Creatures,
      Come Christmas the morn!
    Little Christ Jesus
      Our brother is born.

Now every Bird that flies in air,
  Sing, raven, lark and dove!
The night has brooded on her lair
  And fledged the Bird of Love.
    Sing sweet as the flute,
      Sing clear as the horn,
    Sing joy of the Birds
      Come Christmas the Morn!
    Little Christ Jesus
      Our brother is born.

A CAROL FOR CHRISTMAS EVE

We come to your doorstep
    To sing you a song,
Our tune is but simple,
    Our voices aren't strong.

We sing of a Baby
    As old as he's new—
Now welcome the Baby,
    And welcome us too.

The Babe had no cradle
    To rock him to rest.
The arms of the Mother
    Rock all babies best.

The Babe had no garment
    Of silk and of gold.
Her own mantle kept him
    Within a blue fold.

The Babe had no mansion
    In which he might roam
He lay on her bosom,
    And that was his home.

Each year as the time comes,
    We too come along
To stand on your doorstep
    And sing you a song.

We sing of a Baby
  This night born anew,
For the sake of the Baby
  God bless me and you.

What will go into the Christmas Stocking
While the clock on the mantelpiece goes tick-tocking?
    An orange, a penny,
    Some sweets, not too many,
    A trumpet, a dolly
    A sprig of red holly,
    A book and a top
    And a grocery shop,
    Some beads in a box,
    An ass and an ox,
    And a lamb, plain and good,
    All whittled in wood,
    A white sugar dove,
    A handful of love,
    Another of fun,
    And it's very near done—
    A big silver star
    On top—there you are!
Come morning you'll wake to the clock's tick-tocking,
And that's what you'll find in the Christmas Stocking.

KEEPING CHRISTMAS

How will you your Christmas keep?
Feasting, fasting, or asleep?
Will you laugh or will you pray,
Or will you forget the day?

Be it kept with joy or pray'r,
Keep of either some to spare;
Whatsoever brings the day,
Do not keep but give away.

THE CHRISTMAS TREE

I set a little Christmas tree
In my workroom just for me,
Hung with many a gleaming thing—
With lines of tinsel shimmering,
And ruby balls and gold were seen,
A trumpet, and two blue-and-green
Glass peacocks, silver nuts as well,
A Father Christmas and a bell.

Then Twelfth Night came. And I took down
The ivy-trails, the holly-crown,
The bunch of pearly mistletoe—
The time was come for all to go.
But looking at my Christmas tree
I thought, 'It seems a shame to me
To put the pretty thing away
When it will yet last many a day.'

And so I took the little pot
Between my hands, and when I got
Outside I went to Perrin's Court
Where little children play and sport.
Tinkling and twinkling on my way
I went, and they all stopped their play
To gaze at my bright Christmas tree,
And 'Oo!' they cried, 'Oo! Ooo!' at me.

So I know how a rocket feels
When in the midst of wondering squeals
Upon its glittering way it goes
And stars upon the heavens sows.
But rockets vanish in the air,
While still my little tree somewhere
Bestows its shining joys on two
Small children who are saying 'Oo!'

In a far land upon a day,
Where never snow did fall,
Three Kings went riding on the way
Bearing presents all.

And one wore red, and one wore gold,
And one was clad in green,
And one was young, and one was old,
And one was in between.

The middle one had human sense,
The young had loving eyes,
The old had much experience,
And all of them were wise.

Choosing no guide by eve and morn
But heaven's starry drifts,
They rode to find the Newly-Born
For whom they carried gifts.

Oh, far away in time they rode
Upon their wanderings,
And still in story goes abroad
The riding of the Kings:

So wise, that in their chosen hour,
As through the world they filed,
They sought not wealth or place or power,
But rode to find a Child.

Just before bed,
'Oh, *one* more story,
Mother!' they said,
And in the glory
Of red and gold
Beyond the fender
Their Mother told
Splendour on splendour.

A small boy threw
A handful of seeds,
And a beanstalk grew
Faster than weeds
As high as heaven . . .
She wore a red hood . . .
Once there were seven
Dwarfs in a wood . . .

So the children found
A gingerbread house . . .
So Puss with a bound
Killed the Giant-mouse . . .
'Now, Mother, tell a
Best tale of all!'
So Cinderella
Went to the ball . . .

'Don't stop, Mother!'
It's time to rest.
'Oh, tell us another,
The *very* best!'
So the best of all
She told to them:
'Once in a stall
In Bethlehem' . . .

A WISH

A glad New Year to all—
Since many a tear,
Do what we can, must fall,
The greater need to wish a glad New Year.

Since lovely youth is brief,
O girl and boy,
And no one can escape a share of grief,
I wish you joy;

Since hate is with us still,
I wish men love,
I wish, since hovering hawks still strike to kill,
The coming of the dove;

And since the ghouls of terror and despair
Are still abroad,
I wish the world once more within the care
Of those who have seen God.

Index of First Lines

159